THE LICH

(OR, THE CONFESSIONS OF A WITCH-KING)

BY

ADAM VINE

COPYRIGHT 2017 ADAM CHRISTOPHER KENNEDY

This work is licensed under a Creative Commons Attribution-Noncommercial-No Derivative Works 3.0 Unported License.

Attribution — You must attribute the work in the manner specified by the author or licensor (but not in any way that suggests that they endorse you or your use of the work).

Noncommercial — You may not use this work for commercial purposes.

No Derivative Works — You may not alter, transform, or build upon this work.

Inquiries about additional permissions should be directed to: theadamvine@gmail.com

Cover Design by Laura Hollingsworth

This is a work of fiction. Names, characters, places, brands, media, and incidents are either the product of the author's imagination or are used fictitiously. Any resemblance to similarly named places or to persons living or deceased is unintentional.

PRINT ISBN: 9798637207916

"Do not meddle in the affairs of wizards, for they are subtle and quick to anger."

J.R.R. Tolkien

They called me the Coffin King.

I was the hero who slew the Lich and returned the Crown of Whispers to the Empire. I was the man of the people who rose to become emperor, only to fall again to a conspirator's blade. I was cursed. I became a creature of darkness, doomed to wander these shadowed halls for years uncounted. I have feasted on the bones of brave warriors, like you, who came by the thousands to win glory to their names through my destruction. I have stolen fair maidens in front of their beloveds' eyes and made them my lifeless brides. I have turned more men to bones than now march in all the armies of the earth. I have learned the songs of death undying. The mere mention of my name sends children to bed at a reasonable hour and keeps them from playing outside after dark.

I am the monster the stories warned you about.

But you already know all this, don't you? Otherwise, you wouldn't have ventured miles beneath the earth to my Castle-Under-The-Mountain, into my Hall of Echoes, to the foot of my Throne of Skulls, silver sword in hand, ready to drive it through my cold, un-beating heart. You wouldn't have slaughtered my wights and left their dust piles littering my halls. You wouldn't have waltzed past every single chest I left for you, brimming with treasures and in plain view, with only booby traps a child could disarm -- a last generous offer for you to turn back. You wouldn't be wearing that same fragile smirk I've seen so many times before, which you assure yourself is an adequate mask for your fear.

You wouldn't have come to slay the Lich if you didn't already know what I am. But there are some minor discrepancies in the popular version of my story, the one you have heard. Inaccuracies. Falsehoods. Naked slander.

Yes, it's true. Those are the bones of your fellow monster hunters scattered beneath the cobwebs of my hall. That mountainous pile of silver swords, spears, axes, glaives, and lances belonged to them.

And yes, I have been sitting here sharpening these long, black fingernails on the skulls of my throne for years uncounted.

Yes, the Crown of Whispers, which you have come to reclaim, does adorn my lolling head, too heavy for my frail neck to hold upright.

Yes, I am the Lich.

But what kind of noble warrior would you be, if you slew me without knowing the entire story? Any man who is willing to become an executioner must first be a good listener, should he not? To be a confidant for the last words of the one he has condemned?

Be honest with yourself. You didn't only come here to plunge your brilliant, glittering blade – no doubt blessed by the Moon Singers with menstrual blood and sacred oils - through the cracked, pale leather of my flesh, to send me at long last to Hell's waiting gates, and take the Crown of Whispers for yourself. You came for a confession… to hear the true account of my un-life, straight from the corpse's mouth. So, a confession you shall have.

But please, come a little bit closer. I don't trust you, either. But we can't get started with you standing halfway across the room. This old, dead voice is only so strong.

I began my life as a coffin maker's son. I was never schooled, except in the art of felling cloud pines and fashioning them into six-foot-long boxes for the dead. My father was the most hated man in our village. It was difficult for me to make friends.

I spent my boyhood exploring the cloud forest where we cut our trees, pretending I was all manners of warriors and royal assassins, even going so far as to spy on the local lord, whose name is now lost to me, and his retainers when they went hawking in my woods. I quickly learned two ways of speaking – one for the people in our village, and one for myself, when I was alone and pretending to be a nobleman.

My father taught me how to survive on my own: which plants and their roots could be eaten and which would kill; how to track deer, rabbits, and squirrels; how to follow without being seen; how to stalk and take aim; how to kill with a single shot.

My father had served as an archer in the king's army before turning to the trade of making coffins. I practiced with his longbow as soon as I was old enough to draw it, at first until my wrists and fingers bled, then when sufficient calluses formed until he deemed I should stop. I learned the differences between hunting for food and hunting in war, how to hold my arrows in my bow hand so I could quick-draw them without reaching for my quiver, how to shape my own bow from yew, or cloud pine if yew wasn't available.

But my father was a drunk and flew into an easy rage at the smallest provocation. If I misplaced a nail or dented the wood with my hammer, he would box my face and sides until he felt something break. If I overshot my target and lost my arrows in the woods, he would not let me eat or sleep under his roof until I found them.

Eventually, I stopped wanting back inside and made myself a bed of pine boughs in a cave high in the cloud forest overlooking our valley, next to the place where the river fell over jagged bluestone cliffs into a deep, crystalline pool.

It was there I met Justina, my first love.

I can still envision her, as if she were here, standing where you are in this very hall. She had hair the color of volcanic glass, eyes that held the light like jade arrowheads. Her face was a pale, heart-shaped jewel, her skin the blue-gold color of fresh milk. When she smiled, it filled my heart with the indescribable mixture of joy and sadness that only comes when we love someone more than we love ourselves.

She was bathing naked in my Crystal Pool at dusk, and her mother caught me watching. Her mother recognized me as the coffin maker's boy and vengefully promised to turn me over to him come the dawn. But I begged and pleaded not to make me go back to him, for he'd beat me bloody, possibly even kill me, the tears carving their own waterfalls from the encrusted dirt and grime of my cheeks. I must have looked an overwhelmingly pitiful creature, because the old bag relented and started crying, too, avowing to take me in.

My father didn't seem much bothered by my new living arrangements. I slept in the attic of the inn owned by Justina's family. In exchange, I washed the guests' dishes, which – on top of my duties at the coffin shop – thankfully only amounted to an hour or two of work each week, since our village was far removed from the roads taken by most travelers.

And so I left my cave by the Crystal Pool and rejoined the village of my birth, albeit, not for long.

When Justina's mother would go to bed, I would steal a bottle of wine from the cellar and Justina would sneak out her window to meet me at the edge of town. Navigating by candlelight, we would sneak up the mountain path to the cloud forest, where we'd get drunk and swim in the Crystal Pool, then fondle each other on my bed of pine boughs until we both fell asleep. As long as we both awoke and were back before dawn, her mother was never the wiser.

Justina was the first girl I ever lay with. But our happiness, like all things, was only a single note in the ceaseless elegy of time.

I caught her fucking the nobleman's son.

I grew nervous the first time he stayed at the inn and saw a look pass between them while she was serving him ale-roasted duck with apples. When he returned a week later, I grew suspicious. The growing knot of sickness in my gut completed its winding when I spied his men out hawking in the forest, but curiously, he wasn't there.

I found him taking her from behind against a tree, not far from our Crystal Pool, where she'd promised she was mine, forever.

I lost many sleepless nights convincing myself it was my fault. Justina told me that I was being stupid. If she married a lord, she could be a lady, and live in a castle, and didn't I want her to be happy? Her words only stoked the fires of my jealousy. On my last night in the village, I recall imagining I was standing over her bed while she slept, dagger in hand, trying to talk myself into slitting her throat.

But in the end, I simply packed what few belongings I had in a potato sack, slung it over my shoulder and stole away upon a moonlit road, promising myself between peaks and troughs of rage and heartbreak that I would use my pain as fuel to see the world and make myself better.

Whatever you may think of me now, dear warrior, there was a time when I was a good man. Now please, come a bit closer. I'm going to strain myself with all this shouting.

I arrived in the capital city of Ito a month later, as lean and weary as the road could make me. It was mid-summer, and the sun was ungodly hot, made worse by the fact there was no water anywhere. The capital was experiencing the worst drought in recorded history. The wells and streambeds were dry. A bath was a luxury, and drinking water had to be purchased from merchants who charged prices so astronomical I wondered how the city's poor could survive.

It was there I saw the truth of the stories I'd been hearing since I was a boy that our once-great Empire was dying.

The fields were barren and the trees were black and brittle. The ancient palaces and grand promenades were filthy and overrun with beggars. Giant columns of unwashed, unpainted stone stained black with smoke towered over swarms of mucky children lying bored and starving in the shade, whose ribs showed through tattered shirts and grubby fingers clawed at my own patch-riddled pants as I passed.

"You're from the provinces. They think you're rich," an impossibly tall, thin merchant said to me with a laugh. He was selling locusts, the one food item the capital seemed to have in abundance. He wore a savagely curled black mustache that covered half his face and mirrored the shape of the dagger hung from his belt.

"Why?" I said.

The merchant responded, "Because life is still good there. The fruits still ripen on the vine. The water is still clear enough to drink. People are healthy, and their bellies are full. But it won't be so for much longer. Soon the corruption destroying this place will spread there, too. He means it to spread over the entire world."

"Who?" I said.

The merchant picked up one of his own locusts and let it hover by his mouth, not noticing the minute tremble of its legs, and said, "The Lich."

A confounded look must have seized my face, for he raised an eyebrow at me and said, "Have you not heard of him?"

"No," I said. "Who, or what, is a Lich?"

With a heaving sigh that trembled the locust's tiny feelers, the merchant began: "He was High Wizard, the Emperor's most valued advisor. He murdered the Emperor and stole the Crown of Whispers, which the gods of Sun and Moon gave to this land in the Age before Time. Rumor has it he used black magic to seduce the Princess. Many believed the High Wizard meant to use her to usurp the throne."

"So, what stopped him?" I said.

The merchant scraped one greasy, shining corner of his mustache with the locust's tail and said, "Because his plot was discovered, and the Emperor had him arrested. But on the morning of his execution, instead of going to his death with honor, the High Wizard murdered the Emperor, stole the Crown of Whispers, and fled to the Castle-Under-The-Mountain."

"Forgive me, but what is the Castle-Under-The-Mountain? You must remember, I'm from the provinces, and don't know much about politics," I said.

"It is an ancient, hidden fortress - a secret redoubt built to hide the royal family in times of crisis," the Merchant said. "No one knows its exact location though many seek to find it. For the Lich remains there still, using the Crown of Whispers to blight this land with famine and plague. Did you do *any* research into our fine city before coming here?"

"News takes long to travel to the provinces," I said.

The merchant shrugged and, at last, popped the unfortunate locust in his mouth, biting down with a loud crunch.

To avoid an uncomfortable silence with my new friend, I pushed the subject, "So why do you call him a… what was it you said? A Lich? What makes him so different from any other run-of-the-mill bastard, philanderer, scoundrel, or brigand?"

Through a mouthful of insect parts, the merchant said, "Because the gods punished the High Wizard for his betrayal. They cursed him, sapping the life from his body. The gods turned him into a living corpse, who must drain the souls of the living to continue existing."

It was my turn to scratch my beard. "If that's true, then shouldn't he already be dead? Or, gone? Or whatever way you want to put it. He secluded himself in a place that sounds very difficult to get to, and he can only survive by preying on others. So it sounds like the problem has solved itself."

The merchant grinned, revealing a mouthful of silver-capped teeth. He offered me a locust. I took it and chewed. It tasted similar to the fried minnows Justina's mother used to serve guests at her inn. "A-ha. Right, you are, my boy. And if no one ever sought him out, you would be correct - the problem would easily sort itself out…

"Unfortunately, or fortunately, depending on your perspective, there seems to be no shortage of brave idiots with silver swords and maidens' promises in hand, eager to march off on a fool's quest to slay the Lich, regain the Crown of Whispers, and save the Empire. There is a widespread belief that whoever kills the Lich and takes the Crown from his head will become the new king."

I shook my head, confused. "But isn't it true that if nobody goes to find him, he won't have any souls to feed on, and would simply vanish?"

The merchant shrugged. "If you ask me, people simply can't resist the temptation to be heroes. It's not only power they want - they want recognition, too. They want to be *right*. We have such a need to feel morally superior to others, that we will go far out of our way to pay attention to those who we despise, even when not doing so would cause our opponents to wither and die from obscurity."

"So you're saying the Lich has an infinite supply of food."

The merchant swallowed his last bite of locust and said: "I can see you're thinking of going after him. I've tried to convince you not to, but I understand the appeal. I can tell you where to begin your search: the map showing the location of the Castle-Under-The-Mountain is hidden in the Great Library. Who knows? Maybe the next time we meet, I'll be calling you *your majesty*."

It wasn't hard to figure out where the map was hidden. I suspected it would be built into some part of the library's architecture, most certainly the floor, so I climbed the stacks until I reached the highest indoor vantage point the library offered, a hanging scaffold where an absent artist had recently been repairing one of the spires in the giant mosaic of the Crown of Whispers that adorned the inside of the dome.

No, the hard part was seeing through all the bodies. Sleeping, standing, leaning, begging, the library floor was teeming with refugees, orphans, and the homeless, who had nowhere else to go. It was the largest building in the capital, even larger than the royal palace, and open to the public. I had to wait until five minutes before closing when the last tawny fingers of dusk were seeping through the highest skylight before I could make out the image on the floor.

The map was, as I'd expected, hidden in the design of the floor tiles. I instantly recognized the landmarks, as they were close to the valley where I'd grown up. The river that gave life to my village was a tributary of the great river Ist, which flowed south from the Iga Mountains, and was the map's starting point. I would have to cross the mountains at the Izo Pass, the sacred high road where the Sisterhood of the Moon Singers lived in their ancient monasteries cut straight from the faces of the rock. Then, I would have to ascend the heights until I found the mountaintop crater holding the lake known as the Eye of the Sea, where the entrance to the Castle-Under-The-Mountain was hidden.

I spent many more days in that library, learning everything I could about Liches, undead curses, and how to defeat them. Since I could not read the books myself, I employed a young girl named Pia to read them to me. Pia had bright, translucent hair the color of whiskey and barely looked old enough to be in school, yet was already studying alchemy at the university level. I paid her in locusts borrowed from the locust merchant, my friend San, on promises that when I came into my empire, he would be my chief advisor. He always gave them to me with a silver-capped smile and a wink.

With Pia's aid, I learned that silver is toxic to the undead, but that they also hoard it. I didn't understand this paradox until my young assistant found in an old black tome that the undead is drawn to silver by instinct, just as we are to food or drink, but it cannot harm them unless it penetrates the heart or brain. Being creatures sustained by magic, the undead can wield magic far easier than mortal humans. Monsters draw their use of magic from silver, but as their ability with magic rises, so does the damage done to them by that most precious of metals. Liches, while exceedingly frail physically, are among the most devastating sorcerers in existence. Thus, their (or should I say, our?) allergy to silver is quite high.

I decided the best way to kill the Lich would be with a silver arrowhead. I had it all figured out: I would sneak into the Castle-Under-The-Mountain and shoot the Lich through his cold, wicked heart, take the Crown of Whispers and be back in Ito before the seasons changed.

I convinced Pia's father, a metalworker named Gahri, to forge me twenty silver arrowheads. He was as strong and skilled with an axe as a blade catcher in the Emperor's royal guard, so I promised he would be my Royal Master-At-Arms when I came into my kingdom.

The next morning at dawn I set out to slay the Lich.

When I entered the Lich's lair, it soon became apparent how little I knew about magic. The old corpse had seen me coming before I had dipped my toes into the Eye of the Sea's icy, glass surface, even before I had left the lowlands for the grueling, week-long climb up the Izo Pass.

Fireballs shot at me from invisible ziggurats secreted in the stones of the walls from my first step into that old, dusty tomb. Their scorching heat singed the hair off my arms and neck as I flailed and ducked to dodge their paths.

I sprinted and slid down serpentine halls of slick, time-smoothed stone, my elk-skin boots barely making a sound as I leaped nimbly over spike pits and impaling objects flung from murder holes in the ceiling and walls, yet the Lich's wights found me as if I wore a beacon. They'd been waiting for me, I knew, as soon as I heard their eager howls echoing from the depths.

You of all people, dear warrior, should know how terrifying it is to be charged by a wight. I can see the sweat still creeping down your brow, the tremble in your fingertips from the vibrations of your sword plunging in and out of eye sockets, ribs, and dead, dusty joints.

I felt it too, back then. The hairs that weren't burned off me stood on end, every inch of my body covered in gooseflesh. My blood flowed like fire, and time, like sugared sludge.

Their dead, contorted lips screeched octaves I didn't think my ears could withstand. I quick-drew my bow on every pale face, every set of flinty, unseeing eyes, unleashing arrow after arrow into the disintegrating slag of their faces, sometimes running at a full sprint or leaping the way my father trained me to. I recovered as many arrows as I could, but by the time I reached this place, this Hall of Echoes, I had only two arrows left.

I crept slowly into the hall, bearing down on every moving shadow, every glimmering mote of dust cascading in the torchlight, but the Lich wasn't there. I stood where you now stand and with great confusion, lowered my bow.

Then I heard him enter, the scraping of rough cloth on smooth stone: *shamble, scratch, shamble, scratch, scratch.* I saw him walking on the ceiling, cupping something in the pallid bowl of his hands.

The Lich uttered a word and I froze. He drifted down as paper falls through the air, silently landing on his throne. He scattered the dust pile he was carrying on the floor. When he spoke, his voice was old and tired, exhaustion seeping through every cough and stutter.

"The gods did not make me a Lich," the Lich said.

I tried to speak and found I could not.

I'm sure you'll agree, dear warrior, that it's hard to describe the look a dead face makes when it emotes. I can only describe it as sadly unsurprised.

The Lich descended his throne and took my face in his hands. His touch stung like ice but was dry as ash. I tried to fight, but I still couldn't move.

I thought he would kill me, but he only wanted to confess.

"My heart stopped beating because it grew cold. Not the other way around. I pushed everyone who ever loved me away for selfish reasons: power, glamor, fame. I mastered the arcane arts. I slew monsters. I did great deeds for king and country, all the while neglecting those who mattered. When I realized just how alone I was, that I would die alone, I desperately sought the purest affection I could find, that of a beautiful young girl with innocence in her eyes. Or did you think I seduced the Princess through magic like everyone else does? You may speak."

"Traitor," I spat. "Murderer. Demon."

He shrugged and returned to his throne, where he tapped a long black fingernail on the bones of the armrest. He was playing with me, I realized, trying to squeeze every last bit of information I knew about the outside world before the end.

But I had no trump card up my sleeve to play against his magic. I couldn't move anything but my lips. My only chance to survive was to make him angry enough to stumble in his routine.

"It is in my nature to be selfish, I suppose. I knew all the right things to say to make her fall in love with me. But in the end, I was afraid to return her love. So I broke the heart of the only girl who could've saved me, for having the audacity to try." The Lich pointed an ebony fingernail at the dust pile at his feet. "These are her ashes, my sweet princess. She was one of the wights you slew coming in."

"What?"

The Lich sighed, dead leaves rattling on dead, dry branches. "She came here, knowing what I was. She begged me to give her the Hymn of Death Undying. In the end, she won. As I said, I'm a selfish creature."

"A fitting end, for one who would murder his own people with famine and plague," I said.

"It's true. The Crown of Whispers is an instrument of tremendous power. You know the legend of how it washed ashore after a great orgy between the Gods of Sun and Moon, and Ithas, the patriarch of this great land, found it and put it on his head. But I can't control it. All I can do is listen to the things it whispers in my ear."

I saw red. "Why tell me this, because you're lonely and consumed by your guilt? What's next? You beg me to take your life, to put you out of your misery, so you feel justified in killing me when I try to?"

For an instant, I felt his grip on me slipping. The invisible pressure on my skin relented, my muscle fibers freed from whatever intangible force had rendered them immobile.

The arrow had left my string before I realized what I'd done. A fireball burst where I had been standing, but my reflexes took control and I rolled away, evading death by a fraction of a second.

When I looked at the Lich again, my silver-headed arrow had impaled the left breast of his tattered purple robes. With an uncoiling hiss, the Lich released his grasp on this world.

Word of my deeds traveled faster than I did. You'd think, my noble warrior, because this is what *you* believe *you* would do, that anyone I met on the road would simply kill me and take the Crown of Whispers for themselves, but it was not so.

As soon as anyone I met learned of what I'd done, they fell at my feet and groveled. A dozen battle-hardened warriors far stronger and more skilled at the fine art of violence than *you* knelt to kiss my boots before I had left the first village, and by the time I departed the mountains, my army was over two thousand strong.

They called me the Coffin King. They told stories around their fires about me, the coffin maker's son who had risked his life to save the land he loved, outsmarted the Lich, and would use the Crown of Whispers to restore life to our dying land.

Men are quick to follow strength, but even quicker to follow stories.

Please, dear warrior. Do come a bit closer. I don't have the strength to continue the story at this volume. Please, just a few steps. There. Good. Now, where was I? Ah, yes: Ito.

I arrived in Ito with ten thousand warriors at my back, each ready to fight to the death to take the capital and carry me to my new throne on their shoulders. But Ito greeted us as heroes, with a grander parade than I ever thought possible. A hundred thousand people lined the streets under the shade of the old arches and columns, the stones all washed and freshly painted for my arrival. Confetti snowed down on our heads as our ears were filled with cries of ecstasy and the ringing of a thousand golden bells.

The city's wells were already filling with fresh, clear water. Late summer blossoms bloomed on branches that had been bare weeks earlier. Grain was sprouting in the fields and fruit from the old vines.

The true death of the Lich had given new life to the Empire.

Here I must pause, my noble, and oh-so-gallant warrior, to make a few observations about you.

First of all, you're timid. Shouldn't it be I who fears you, not the other way around?

Second, your dress and posture show you come from humble origins, as I did. Not a coffin maker's son; the strength of your upper back tells me you were a farmer's boy, probably raised by your uncle.

Third, you fight for love, hoping your deeds will win her back. What was her name? Ah, Lina, was it? We shall remember that.

Fourth, you are disgusted by me, and yet simultaneously intrigued. You wonder how a thing that appears so weak could hold such power.

Fifth, you wonder how you will get this crown off my head; if you will have cut it off where the flesh has grown over and entwined with the spires; if you will have the strength left to carry it.

I assure you all your questions will be answered in time.

Now, please, come a bit closer.

I did not put on the Crown of Whispers until my coronation, fourteen days after I re-entered the capital. While on the road, I had carried it in my rucksack, though the weight of it and the sharpness of its spires tore through the rough spun cloth so many times I eventually had to put it inside a second sack, then a third, so it wouldn't fall out.

My coronation was hailed as the greatest party the Empire had ever seen. I swore an oath on the steps of the Great Library before the Sun Father, the Moon Mother, and the people of Ito.

I appointed my friend San, the locust merchant, as my High Wizard, the most important political advisor in the Empire. I appointed Pia's father, the brutish, axe-wielding metalsmith named Gahri, as my Master-At-Arms. I appointed a dozen other members of my court whose names and qualifications came at the highest recommendation from the incumbents.

A grand feast was held for the commoners on Library Plaza, and a more private affair for the members of my court in the tea gardens within the palace walls.

It was there that San, the former locust merchant, approached me and said, "The crown suits you. But I think it's a bit of a farce for anyone to call me a High Wizard when I don't know the first thing about magic."

"We'll learn together. I've already ordered every book and scroll belonging to the former High Wizard to be delivered to my chambers," I said.

"I suppose you should be an expert, having killed the most powerful sorcerer in the Empire," San said.

"The Lich yearned for true death because it was the only thing that could silence his guilt."

San took a long survey of the feast-goers sauntering about the flower ponds and moss-speckled bridges of the garden. The topic clearly made him uncomfortable.

"You know they will expect you to take a wife before the harvest," he said. "Now that the Crown of Whispers has been found, the Empire is even less secure than before it was lost. The Old Families consider you an upstart, and won't think twice about cutting your throat in your sleep so one of their own can take your place. You need a powerful alliance made through marriage to secure your position. Even then, I would not trust anyone who didn't know you back when you had nothing but the patches in your pants."

San gave me his best silver-capped grin and offered me a locust. "Try one yet? They're my favorite. Dipped in chocolate."

I saw her dancing with one of the courtier's daughters under the starlight during the band's last waltz, on the marble balcony astride the grand ballroom of the palace.

She was Justina come again. She had the same crow-colored hair and burnished jade eyes, the same bridge of freckles over her nose, the same elegant spill of good hips and spider-slim legs. She was taller than Justina, older as well, but I couldn't shake the feeling that the woman dancing in front of me was Justina's shade.

The music died and the dance floor cleared. We looked at each other and she started laughing. I was shy, but a healthy swig of wine quickly emboldened me.

"Your highness did not ask me to dance," the woman who was not Justina said.

"A king doesn't need to ask."

She placed a white-gloved hand on my arm and said, "But apparently he needs wine to be able to speak to his subjects."

"What is your name?"

"I'll only tell you if you dance with me."

"I could throw you in the dungeon for that."

"Maybe I want you to."

Reluctantly, I took her hands and led her to the dance floor. I was always a horrible dancer – girls in my village would laugh in my face when I asked them to dance at the Juvenalia - but the wine and the weight of the Crown upon my head let me momentarily forget it.

Oh, you think that's funny, do you, dear warrior? I'm sure a strong, handsome farmer's boy like you never embarrassed himself in front of the girls, oh no, surely not. Why else would you be off on some fool's quest to impress one? Ah, there it is. I see it in your eyes. You're an even worse dancer than I was.

But the woman who was not Justina did not punish me for my missteps. She only smiled and introduced herself. "I am the Lady Ita, of the Water Lily House. I see you have taken a pine tree as your sigil. Does that mean you are sturdy and strong? Or only that you are prickly, and have a strong scent?"

"Neither. It means I came from the earth and will soon return to it. All that matters is what I leave behind."

"Not many kings are also great poets."

"So, where is your lord husband, Lady Ita? Forgive me. I was only a coffin maker's son before… this. I don't know much about politics," I said.

"Don't worry. He's been dead seven years."

"I'm sorry."

"Was it hard, going from pauper to king?"

"No. Strange perhaps, but not hard… at least, not yet. The only way I can describe it is like being a visitor at your own dinner table."

"You know, you don't speak like a coffin maker's son," the Lady Ita said.

"And you don't speak like a lady in mourning."

"Maybe I'm not a lady in mourning, anymore."

"Nor am I still a coffin maker's son."

A month later, we were wed.

The Empire entered a period of extended peace.

I left most of the actual ruling to my councilors, preferring to spend my time studying every book, scroll, and diary I could find on the subject of magic. Most were pilfered from the old High Wizard's study. Some, I had Pia fetch me from the Great Library.

I locked myself in my chambers through all hours of the day and night, breaking only to sign royal edicts, eat, sleep, and make love to my new queen. I consumed all that I could about magic, its uses, counters, history, and secrets.

Now that I had the Crown of Whispers, I was determined to keep it. San's advice had never steered me wrong. I immediately saw plots developing among the Old Families. The cook was an agent of the Redwood House; the girl who changed my linens, a spy for the Roses; my Queen's favorite handmaid, a skilled assassin of the Orchids in disguise.

One of the Crown's magical attributes was that it could dictate what I saw written on the page, directly into my ear. Any text that didn't make sense to me, the Crown paraphrased in a way that did. The Crown helped me master the pronunciation of difficult spells. The Crown taught me to read, which - for a boy who grew up making coffins - felt just as magical as the balls of fire or lightning I formed in my hands. I became the Crown's pupil.

Magic is often nothing more than finely crafted illusions enhanced by the manipulation of chemical reactions which produce certain desired, often explosive effects. The ziggurats which shot their scorching balls of fire at me when I entered the Castle-Under-The-Mountain, for example, were nothing more than arrows tipped with high-combustion fuel rigged to fire when someone stepped on a carefully hidden pressure plate. So, too, did the Crown teach me to use illusions to my advantage.

After two years, I had learned everything the old High Wizard had known and more. The Lich's spells, which had so dazzled and terrified me when I entered his dank fortress, seemed nothing more to me now than the cheap tricks of a parlor flop. The Crown was true power.

My queen was patient and loving until she wasn't. She grew cruel and icy at a word. Any perceived slight became a screaming match that shook the tapestries from the walls and sent our servants running from our chambers with flushed cheeks and averted eyes.

She caught me staring at the linen girl and accused me of cheating.

She accused me of not loving her.

She accused me of thinking she was old and ugly.

She accused me of abandoning her, of never spending time with her, of not actually studying, but spending time with other women.

At last, I grew so furious that I slapped the wine cup from her lips and my queen ran from the room, crying. I spent the night alone in my solar, getting so drunk I woke up the next afternoon in a pool of my own vomit.

After that night, on the rare occasions when I ventured out of my study to see my queen, she would kiss me, service me, and lay on the bed with her legs apart. But when the deed was done, we would part ways and each return to our separate chambers.

Three years into my rule, an alliance of bandit tribes in the Iga Mountains declared independence from the Empire. My advisors had predicted as much, since that region had never truly accepted imperial rule.

They butchered my emissaries and sent their heads back on silver-tipped arrows.

You must make an example of them, or others will follow, the Crown whispered to me.

I led a raiding party to the Izo Pass, where we slaughtered the bandits in their camp while they slept. I put three silver-tipped arrows through their leader's heart, then cast a flurry of flame and ice down upon their heads so cruel they threw down their weapons and surrendered at my feet.

The Crown was not appeased. *They defied you*, it whispered. *Rebellion is in their blood. You must wipe it from the earth, every man, woman, and child.*

I gave the order. We left none alive.

My cruelty to the Mountain People did not go unnoticed back home in the capital. A series of anonymous pamphlets began circulating bearing the words *KILLER OF WOMEN AND CHILDREN!* And *NO HEIR!*

I consulted my councilors, who agreed the Old Families had put out the libelous filth. San, my High Wizard, told me, "People are quick to trash talk their leaders, and even quicker to believe the slander they hear. This is just politics as usual."

My Master-At-Arms, Gahri was less optimistic. "Soon they will rise against you. They saw you as a hero for saving them from the Lich, but stories die. It's unfortunate your legend faded so quickly, but that's how it is. There's talk in the streets the queen cannot conceive. You need to give the people something new to put their hope in. You need to give them an heir."

But, try as I did, my queen's belly never swelled. I shot my seed upon her thighs or stomach. I didn't want it. Not with her.

By my fifth year, the Empire was the most prosperous it had ever been.

To bolster my public image, I threw wild, lavish festivals, bacchanalias complete with beautiful dancers, fire summoners, elephants, succulent feasts, and gladiatorial games that lasted weeks at a time. I built monuments to myself on every street corner and square, replacing statues of the gods with ones of myself fighting the Lich. I started construction on a new temple fashioned with my own face equal in size and splendor to the Great Library. I ordered a fleet of one thousand ships built, promising pioneering families free passage to the New Provinces. I sought to spread my dominion beyond the setting sun.

I spent the nights getting drunk on the best wines ever fermented and enjoying the most beautiful whores the world had ever seen.

And then there were the campaigns. I suppressed three more bandit rebellions in the Iga Mountains – rebellions I fomented, of course, by staging false flag ambushes on my own troops. Thousands died. The army began its push to expand the imperial borders to the north and south, on the pretense of protecting the settlers from the bloodthirsty natives. The body count climbed to the tens, then to the hundreds of thousands.

Yes, my gallant warrior. You've heard of those wars, haven't you? You learned of my wars in the Borderlands as ancient history. But the people in the New Provinces still hate the Empire for the brutality our soldiers showed there. Mass murder. Crucifixions. Infanticide.

And now I know something else about you, my wight-slaying friend: you're a bookworm. No wonder you look so nervous with a blade. Please, come a little closer.

I fell in love with my own story anew each morning when I looked in the mirror. The Crown affirmed me: *You are a good king*, it whispered. *The people love you. You have saved the Empire. You are a good king, but not a great one. Your queen is holding you back.*

I had the queen's chambers moved to the farthest tower of the palace, sending the message by courier since I didn't have time to do it face-to-face. I was with an eighteen-year-old whore who could have been Justina's twin. The queen didn't remind me of her anymore. She'd grown saggy and old.

I never spoke to the Lady Ita again.

In the tenth year of my reign, I divorced the Lady Ita and banished her to the Sisterhood of the Moon Singers to marry Pia, my young former assistant.

Nearly a decade had passed since I'd last seen her. Gahri showed up at one of my garden parties with a stunningly pretty young woman on his arm, who I didn't recognize. It wasn't until my Master-At-Arms grew visibly nervous that I realized the girl was Pia.

She'd grown into a woman of breathtaking beauty. She was slender and almond-eyed with a radiant smile and hair so blonde it gleamed like silver in the late afternoon light. I learned that Gahri had sent her away to study alchemy at the New University in the Southern Province. He introduced her as "The Lady Pia," and sweated so profusely while doing so I thought he would drown in his own shirt.

Pia only grinned, offered me her hand to kiss, and said, "I hope you still love stories, your highness. I've brought you many, many great books."

We wed in the Great Library at sunset on the Feast of the Sacred Crown, standing where we'd first met over a decade earlier, among the stacks beneath a dozen shades of sanguine falling through the high stained-glass windows like a story fractured in the retelling. I promised Pia I would be hers forever, and she would be mine.

And the Crown whispered: *But we've heard that before, haven't we?*

Our happiness faded as quickly as it came. I started losing my mind.

The Empire had entered a rapid decline. A decade of war and rampant expansionism had not only drained the gold from the vaults faster than the royal accountants could measure, but had sent many of the Empire's best minds abroad to the New Provinces, where they wouldn't be persecuted.

I, in my infinite wisdom, had begun executing any academics or members of the Old Families who spoke out against me, burning them alive on the steps of the Great Library as traitors.

My councilors grew distant. The tenuous friendships I'd formed with San and Gahri withered. I stopping heeding their counsel, and eventually they stopped giving it, choosing to spend our meetings staring blankly into their wine cups instead.

My popularity with the public hit an all-time low. Vicious rumors surfaced that despite still not having a legitimate heir, I'd sired hundreds of deformed bastards upon countless whores across various regions of the Empire. The former, at least, was true. Pia and I tried to produce a child, but like the queen who preceded her, Pia's belly never grew.

Whatever sliver of control I'd had over my temper with the Lady Ita vanished completely when Pia and I quarreled. A questioning look would send me spiraling into the foulest of moods; a disagreeing word, and I would rage. I drank the palace dry. And Pia, for all her innocent patience, grew ever more hurt by my pitiless anger. She would lock herself in our bedchamber for hours, crying and begging me to be myself again.

But that was the problem. I was myself. I was a liar, and a whoremonger, and a loner, and a fraud. The only real power I ever had came from the Crown.

I can hear its whispers even now: *We are as they made us, are we not?*

Nothing I did could change my and Pia's fate. The affection she had so selflessly showered upon me in the beginning evaporated with each successive tear. I emptied the royal coffers to take her on exotic trips to the farthest outskirts of the Empire. We spent our nights crying uncontrollably in each other's arms on the sea of satin pillows that adorned the interior of our wheelhouse, until finally, she would place a tender hand on my cheek, and say, "I have loved you since I was a girl, and you were a pauper in rags. Nothing in the world could diminish my love for you now."

And the Crown would whisper in my ear: *You are a fool if you believe her.*

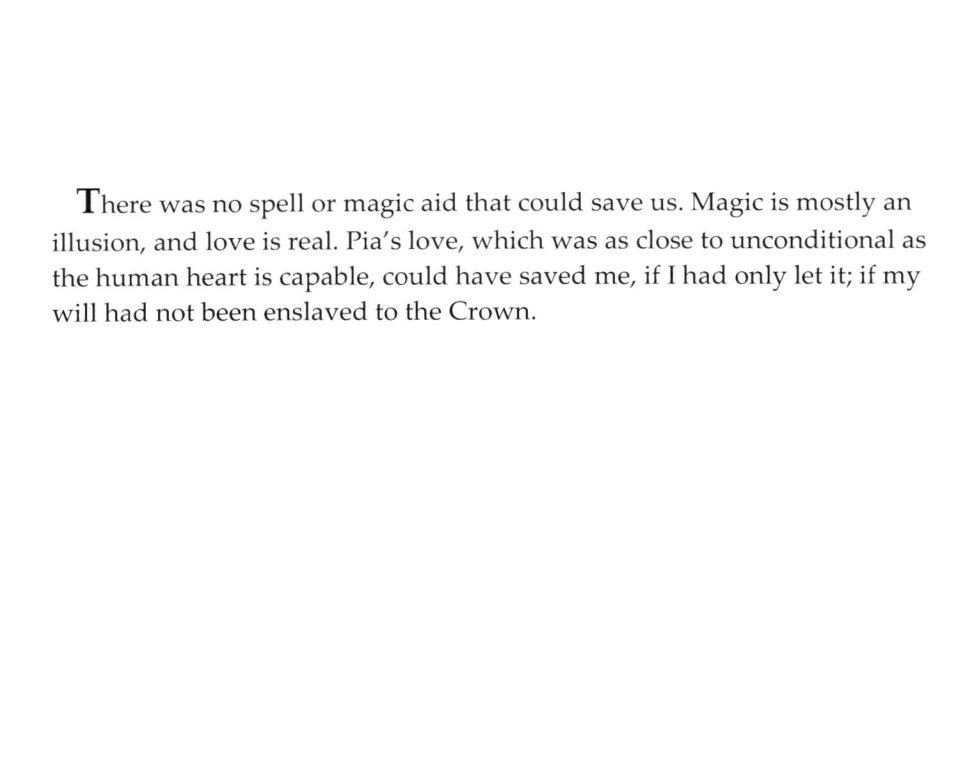

There was no spell or magic aid that could save us. Magic is mostly an illusion, and love is real. Pia's love, which was as close to unconditional as the human heart is capable, could have saved me, if I had only let it; if my will had not been enslaved to the Crown.

I began to suspect the Crown was evil, not a jewel-encrusted diadem at all, but a sentient parasite, and that it was manipulating all of us: me, Pia, our court, and through us, the Empire. I theorized that the Lich I had slain was nothing more than its guardian, a dead, rotten corpse with no will or mind of its own.

The Crown told me I was wrong. But I started having vivid, waking dreams. I ceased being able to tell what was real and what was an illusion.

I dreamt I was a very old man, older than time itself, sitting upon a throne made of skulls, where I slept and waited, sharpening my long, murderous black fingernails to a razor's edge.

I dreamt that my life wasn't mine at all, but someone else's, a story being whispered in my ear by the Crown, which had been sitting so long and heavy upon my head it had fused with my flesh and become part of me. Warriors would come to slay me, not knowing I was only the shell through which the Crown acted, that I could not control my own body, that I could only wait, and watch, and scream inside the silent prison of my mind in cacophony with a thousand other nameless voices.

Inevitably, I would lure those brave warriors in until they came just close enough, then my nails would plunge through their breastplates, chain mail, flesh, bone, and all, driving straight into their still-beating hearts, and those who came to slay me would die. Then I – or rather, the Crown – would absorb their memories, and I would become someone else. I would change into the last warrior who died.

Then I would wake in my chambers, and I was myself again. But this dream came to me so often that part of me started to believe it. I came to believe that the dream where I was a dead man sitting on that old chair having my strings pulled by the Crown was my real life, and my life in the royal palace in Ito was the dream, and always had been; that I'd never been a coffin maker's son.

One night, she tried to take the Crown from me.

I stirred from my dream of being the Lich to find Pia's fingers crawling along the pale edges of my scalp where the Crown joined my head. I hit her hands away and said, "What are you doing?"

"You n-n-never t-take it off," Pia said through stutter-stop sobs. "Look what it's done to you… to us. Please. I want you to take it off, this once. Please."

My voice, magnified by the Crown, thundered so loud it shook the palace to the foundations. "Why should I take it off? I took it from the Lich. I saved the Empire. It chose me! Why should I let you have it?"

Pia trembled, hands raised over her face as though I would strike her. "I d-don't want it, your highness. It's just that…"

My queen hesitated. "I t-tried to take it off twice before, while you were s-sleeping, and couldn't. I thought there might be a latch, but… how *do* you take it off, my love? Your forehead has grown so white. It stinks. I tried to wash it, but… why do you never pray? You neglect the gods. You never let me read to you anymore. I'm worried sick about you."

I do not know if it was I, or the Crown, who said, "If I take it off, we lose everything. Would you sacrifice your Empire and the People to save our marriage, you selfish little whore?"

Pia fell to her knees, weeping and grasping my hand like it was her last shred of life. "My love, do you not see? It's called the Crown of Whispers because *it lies*."

She was a benevolent queen, an adoring wife, and of far greater intelligence than I ever was. Pia saw the writing on the wall before it was written.

I was at court when they came for me. Twenty men of my own household guard surrounded me at spear point, led by Gahri, my Master-At-Arms. Pia, my betrayer, and the last person in this world who could have saved me, wasn't there.

"You, the King, stand convicted of high treason, as well as blasphemy, fraud, adultery, and unholy sodomy. The Sun Father, Moon Mother, their respective churches, and the patriarchs of all the Old Families support these charges. The Queen, the Lady Pia formerly of the Papyrus House, has testified in a secret tribunal that you are mad, and that you have willingly set the Empire of the Sun and Moon on a course towards poverty and destruction.

"Should you sign this confession and admit your crimes, you will be stripped of all wealth and titles, but allowed to spend your life in exile, in the New Provinces. Should you resist, or deny these charges, you will be executed by burning at dawn tomorrow, as your own laws have decreed to be the punishment for treason."

Gahri offered me the parchment to sign. I took it in my hands, ready to tear it in two and then kill them all when I felt hot breath on my neck and heard a familiar voice whisper over my shoulder.

"Don't be a fool," San, my High Wizard, said. "Sign it. Don't throw your life away."

He felt me moving and tried to imprison me with magic, but I had surpassed his parlor tricks years before. The counter to that particular spell, called "Cage of Ice," was one of the first spells I ever learned, a simple spray of grounded lightning.

I impaled San's heart with his own dagger as he fried in a pool of his own magic water, then rained fire and ice down upon my would-be captors, magical traps I'd set ages before in case such an event ever came to pass. The Crown had been right.

They burned and froze and shattered and died, all but Gahri, who dodged my attacks nimbly and rushed me with his long axe. I saw the silver-tipped polearm slashing towards me and remembered the Lich's black fingernails that would have pierced my heart if I hadn't been quick. I slid to Gahri's left and bashed his skull in with mine, using the Crown of Whispers to turn his head into a leaking red pulp.

Then I ran.

And now, dear warrior, you know the story of my fall, of how the unlikely ruler of the greatest Empire known to history lost everything, betrayed by the people he trusted most. You know the rest of my story. I fled into the mountains and became the Lich.

Now, I'm exhausted and find I do not have the strength to speak much longer. Please, come a little closer.

I fled the royal palace to the river, then to the Iga Mountains, then across the Izo Pass and into the heights, to the Eye of the Sea, and the only place I knew I could be alone, the Castle-Under-The-Mountain.

I set traps. I sent out spies, bugs and worms and crows, beasts I could easily control with the Crown's magnetic thrum. I began to change. The Crown changed me. I called out to my bastard children in their dreams. They came to me and became my wights.

I am old and weak as rotten paper. See my lolling head. I can barely hold the Crown aloft. My magic is naught but a bare illusion, no match for your gods-given goodness. You will take the Crown of Whispers for yourself, and return to your Empire, a hero. They will call you "The Farmer King," the boy who killed the Lich, who rose from nothing to save an empire. You will succeed where I failed.

But before you do, a warning:

To be the hero, you must slay the Lich. But to slay the Lich is to slay yourself, for in every man a Lich lies waiting. All that must happen for the Lich to be born is the man must lose everything, and behold, the warrior becomes what he set out to so gallantly kill, as I did, as you will.

So, what are you waiting for, my brave and valiant warrior? Take pity on my bitter, tortured soul. Put me out of my misery. Come nice and close, and strike me down.

Have at me.

They called me the Farmer King.

I was the hero who slew the Lich and returned the Crown of Whispers to the Empire. I was the man of the people who rose to become emperor, only to fall again to a conspirator's blade. But you already know all this, don't you?

Please, come a little bit closer.

Made in United States
Troutdale, OR
02/16/2024

17633253R10027